Eggs and Dan

Story by Beverley Randell
Illustrations by Isabel Lowe

Rigby®

A Harcourt Achieve Imprint

www.Rigby.com
1-800-531-5015

"Can you find some food for us today?"
said Mother Bear.
"Can you get
a basket of eggs, please?"

Father Bear and Baby Bear
went to look for eggs.
They looked down in the grass.

Baby Bear saw a nest.
"Here are some little brown eggs,"
he said.

"Oh dear," said Father Bear,
"the eggs have a bad smell.
They are too old."

"We can't eat bad eggs,"
said Baby Bear.

"We can't go home
without some food,"
said Father Bear.

They walked on, down the hill.

Then Baby Bear said,
"My nose can smell flowers."

"Yes," said Father Bear,
"I can smell flowers, too."

"I can see yellow ones,"
said Baby Bear. "Look!"

"The yellow flowers are dandelions,"
said Father Bear.
"They are good to eat."

"We can go home
with a basket of **dandelions**
for Mother Bear," said Baby Bear.

"Father Bear, come here!

I can see a nest!"

shouted Baby Bear.

"It has a lot of eggs in it."

"They are **good** ones, too,"

said Father Bear.

"Now we have dandelions
and eggs for Mother Bear,"
said Baby Bear.